STORIES BETWEEN US

Cheryl Brown

WOVEN LORE PUBLISHING

For my littles,
the cause of, and delay of, all writing.

ALL WE COULDN'T KEEP

There was a quiet that morning that didn't belong.

Not the kind that comes before the sun rises, when everything is still tucked into itself. This was different. The air felt open in a way it shouldn't have been, like something had slipped out during the night and hadn't come back.

I stood there longer than usual before opening the coop, waiting, maybe, for a sound that didn't come. No soft shifting. No low, sleepy clucks. No impatient scratching against the wood.

Just quiet.

I opened the door anyway. It felt like something you do with your hands when your mind hasn't caught up yet, like reaching for a light switch in a room you've already realized is empty.

The hinges made more noise than usual, or maybe it was just that there was nothing to soften it. Inside, the space felt wrong. Not messy. Not broken. Just... missing something.

I didn't step in right away. I stood at the threshold, looking at a place I knew well enough to notice what wasn't there before I could name it. And then I started counting...

Not out loud.

Just the way you do when you already know the number won't come out right.

...mornings are usually louder than this...

The boys are up before I am most days. Feet down the hallway, doors opening and closing, someone always asking for something before I've had a chance to step outside. And out here, there's always been sound. A kind of steady living noise—clucks layered over each other, wings shifting, the soft scratch of feet against dirt. Small things, but constant. Enough that you don't notice it.

Until it's gone.

I stepped inside then, slow, like moving might change something if I wasn't careful. The ground felt the same under my boots. Packed dirt. Familiar. But there were things out of place in a way I couldn't ignore anymore.

A feather caught against the edge of the nesting box. Another near the door.

Not unusual on their own. There are always feathers somewhere.

But not like this. Not scattered. Not... left.

I took another step in, and then I stopped.

It wasn't one thing. It was the way everything no longer moved around it. The stillness had a shape now. Where there should have been shifting, there was none. Where there should have been small, restless life, there was only space.

I felt it before I let myself see it—that something had ended here.

My hands stayed at my sides. I didn't reach for anything. Didn't rush forward. There's a moment where you understand something fully and still don't want to touch it. I stood there, counting again without meaning to. But this time the numbers didn't just fall short.

They stopped.

And there was no way to make them continue.

For a while, I didn't move. Not because I didn't know what to do, but because doing it would make it real in a way that standing there hadn't yet. Eventually, my body decided before I did. A step forward, then another, careful like the ground might give something back if I didn't press too hard. I bent down without thinking, the way I always do when I reach for them. Routine doesn't ask questions. It just continues.

My hands paused before touching anything, just above, like I could still choose not to. Like there was a version of this moment where I stood back up and everything returned to how it was supposed to be.

But there wasn't.

So I kept going. Slowly. Gently. The way you handle something that mattered. I didn't rush it. Didn't look too closely. Just did what needed to be done, one small movement at a time. There's a quiet kind of work in moments like this. No words. No sound. Just the understanding that something has to be carried.

And no one else is there to carry it but you.

I kept moving, one small thing at a time, not thinking too far ahead. Just the next step, and then the next. But the questions came anyway.

How did this happen?

I didn't say it out loud. Didn't need to. It was already there, sitting just behind everything I was doing. I looked at the latch without meaning to. It was closed. Or at least, it looked like it had been.

Maybe I hadn't set it right. Maybe I had. I tried to remember the night before—what I had done, how it had felt, if there had been anything different. Nothing stood out. Which somehow made it worse. I should have checked again. The thought came sharper than the others.

I should have known...

My hands kept moving, but slower now, more careful, like there was something I could still correct if I just paid enough attention.

They trusted me...

I let that thought stay. Not because I wanted to, but because it felt like something I shouldn't push away. I finished what I could, or maybe just enough that I couldn't stay inside any longer. The air outside felt different when I stepped out. Not fresher. Just...wider. Like everything had more space than it should.

I closed the door behind me without thinking, my hand resting on the wood a second longer than usual. Then I turned, my eyes going straight to the fence. I hadn't planned to look. My body just did. Walking the edge slowly, I followed the line I knew by heart. Post to post. Wire to wire. Nothing at first. Everything where it should be.

Which didn't make sense...

I kept going. A little farther down, near the corner where the ground dips just enough after a good rain, there it was. Not large. Not obvious. Just enough. The wire bent slightly in, the bottom edge lifted where something had pushed through and then moved on.

I stood there, looking at it longer than I needed to, like if I stared hard enough, I might see it happen in reverse. Might understand it. Might find the exact moment where I could have stopped it. I crouched down and pressed the wire back into place, more firmly this time, checking the ground beneath it, the edges, the latch again, even though I already had.

Everything tighter now. More secure... but...too late.

I stayed there for a moment longer, my hand still on the wire. Then I stood up. There wasn't anything left to fix. Only something to remember.

I walked back toward the house slower than I had come out. Nothing had changed. The same path. The same morning light stretching across the yard. The same door waiting at the end of it.

Inside, I could already hear the boys. Feet moving. A cabinet opening. Someone calling for something they couldn't reach...

Life, continuing.

I paused at the door for a second, my hand resting on the handle, just long enough to feel the difference. Then I went in.

"Mom—"

The word came quick, like it always does. I answered the same way I always do. Moved through the kitchen. Reached for what was needed. Opened, handed, wiped, turned. Everything exactly as it had been. Only I carried something now that hadn't been there before. And there wasn't anywhere to set it down.

In the days that followed, nothing settled all at once. It shifted. Small things at first. More movement than usual. Shorter patience between them. Little scuffles that hadn't been there before. Tension, sitting just under the surface. It was easy to tell that they all felt it too. I stayed closer those mornings, watched a little longer than I used to, listened for things I wouldn't have noticed before.

Everything felt thinner. More aware.

And then, slowly, other things began to stand out. One of the hens moved differently now. Careful, but not uncertain. She stayed close to the edges at first, having lost an eye during the attack, she turned her head more often, adjusting to her new life. And he was there with her. The sweet, quiet rooster with the limp. Always a step behind or beside. Never far.

I watched them longer than I meant to. The way he slowed to her pace, without thinking. The way she didn't pull away. This was new. He had never really had hens that stayed near him. Maybe the hens never saw him as a protector. But she, even with only one eye, stayed.

Like she still saw him clearly. Like he had been enough this whole time...

They moved together in a quiet way. Not drawing attention. Not asking for it. Just... choosing each other. As I stood there, watching them, something in me was settling that hadn't been able to before. Not because anything had been fixed. In fact, nothing had. But because something else had taken shape in its place.

Something quieter.

Something I might have missed, if everything had stayed the same. I looked out over what remained. Fewer than before...Changed. Still moving. Still choosing...

And I understood then, not everything we're given is ours to keep. But that doesn't mean nothing stays. Some things deepen. Some things find each other. Some things become more because of what was lost.

I checked the latch one more time before heading back toward the house, the same way I always do now. And as I walked away, I could still hear them behind me. Not as full. But enough.

Enough to know they were still there.

Enough to keep going.

A Different Measure of Time

There were so many forms.

I don't remember what most of them asked. Only that every question felt like it was trying to place something that didn't quite fit. Check here if your child does this. Circle if they don't. Rate from one to five. I sat there longer than I needed to on some of them. Not because I didn't know the answers. But because none of the answers listed felt like the right ones.

Around me, other parents filled theirs out quickly. Pages turning. Pens moving without hesitation. I wondered if it felt clearer for them—if their answers lined up with what was being asked, if there was a version of this where everything made more sense.

I turned the page and kept going.

One question at a time.

That seemed to be the only way through it.

At first, it just felt like a phase of things. Appointments to schedule. Calls to make. Paperwork to send in. A few extra steps added into days that already had their own rhythm. Nothing permanent. Just something to move through.

I kept thinking that...That once we got through this part, things would settle again. That there was a version of normal waiting on the other side of it. So I moved through it the same way I moved through everything else— one thing at a time. Forms turned in. Appointments kept. Notes taken. Questions asked, even when I wasn't sure how to ask them.

Days filled up without looking like they had...

Time passed, but not in the way I was used to measuring it. Not by milestones. Not by progress you could easily point to. Just...movement. Small things. Subtle things. Things that mattered, but didn't always show themselves right away.

Other people's lives kept moving in ways I could see. Plans being made. Trips being taken. Schedules settling into something predictable. Days opening up in ways that made room for other things. I noticed it more than I meant to. Not in a way that made me resent it.

Just... aware.

Like watching something happen at a distance and realizing you weren't moving in the same direction anymore.

Our days didn't open up. They filled. In ways I hadn't planned for. In ways that didn't leave much space between one thing and the next, even when it didn't look like much was happening at all. And somewhere in the middle of it, without deciding to, I stopped measuring time the way I used to.

I stopped asking how far along we were. Stopped comparing what hadn't happened yet. Because it didn't fit anymore. None of it did. There were moments I still felt it, though. That quiet question.

Am I behind?

It didn't come loudly. It never does. It showed up in small ways—passing thoughts, quick comparisons, a glance at what someone else was doing, where they were going, how their days seemed to unfold with a kind of ease I no longer recognized. And then it would pass. Because there was always someone else that needed me. Someone right in front of me. Someone that didn't wait for answers like that.

There were times I still tried to hold onto the shape of things as they had been. Ideas I hadn't let go of yet. Trips we would take. Days that would open up. Time that would feel like mine again in the way I remembered.

I would think about it in small ways at first. Looking ahead, trying to find a place where it might fit. But the more I tried to place it, the more I could feel the edges of it not lining up. Not because it was impossible. Just because it asked for something different than what our days could give. There was always something to consider. Something to plan around. Something that didn't move easily from one place to another.

Even the idea of rest came with effort. And after a while, without deciding to, I stopped reaching for those things the same way. Not in a way that felt like giving up...

Just...letting go of something that no longer fit in my hands.

Time alone became something similar. Not gone. Just changed. It didn't come in hours, or any regular measure of time, anymore. It showed up in smaller spaces—quiet moments between things, pauses that didn't look like much from the outside. I learned to recognize them. To use them when they came. To let them be enough.

And somewhere in all of it, the question started to fade. Not answered...just quieter. Because I was no longer standing still, trying to figure out where I should be. I was already somewhere. And I was right in the middle of it.

There were moments it pressed in more than others. Not loudly. Just enough to be felt. A question asked in passing. A look that lingered a second too long. The kind of well-meaning suggestions that didn't quite understand what they were asking for.

"Have you tried…?"

"Maybe if you just…?"

I would nod sometimes. Smile when it felt easier than explaining. Because the truth didn't always fit into a quick answer. There are things you can guide. And things you can't rush. Things that look simple from the outside, but aren't. There are things that don't move just because you want them to or because someone else thinks they should. Because the timeline says they're supposed to.

I learned that slowly.

Not all at once.

Some mornings, I stood in the same space with three very different rhythms unfolding at the same time. The middle child, moving forward with ease. Steps falling into place without much effort. Routine settling in naturally. And the youngest, they're somewhere in between needing help and gaining independence. But the oldest... not there yet. Not because he wouldn't be. Just because he wasn't. And there was no way to push against that, without pushing against him.

There's a kind of letting go that doesn't feel like giving up. It feels like understanding. Like stepping out of a pace that was never yours to keep. Like choosing to meet someone where they are, instead of pulling them toward where you thought they should be. I stopped explaining it as much after a while. Not because I didn't care to. But because I didn't need to hold it up for anyone else to understand.

I already did.

And in that space, something shifted. Not outside of us. But in the way I saw it. In the way I held it. The noise around us didn't stop. I just stopped listening the same way.

One afternoon, we sat together without much happening. No appointment to get to. No form waiting to be filled out. No next step already lined up. Just a moment that hadn't been claimed yet.

He leaned into me in that way that doesn't ask for anything.

Just presence.

Just closeness.

And I sat there with him, not thinking about what hadn't happened or what might come next. Not measuring the day against anything outside of it. Just...being there. And it felt like something I hadn't been looking for. Something I might have missed, if I had been. I rested my hand over his and stayed where I was. Not moving forward. Not falling behind. Just here.

Together.

Time didn't feel lost anymore, just measured differently.

IT WAS THERE, ALL ALONG

It didn't feel like freedom.

That's what people call it sometimes, when something ends before you were ready for it to. A softer word for something that doesn't feel soft at all. I carried it that way for a few days. Not heavy enough to stop everything, but present enough to sit behind it. Plans that had been there weren't anymore. Time had opened up, but not in a way I had asked for. And I found myself filling it with thoughts that didn't go anywhere useful.

Mostly about people.

About how quickly things shift. How easily you can be set aside. How little control you have over something you thought was steady. How unfair it can all feel. It narrowed things. Made everything feel a little more distant than it had been before, and initially I enjoyed that distance.

After a few days of that, I went out for a walk. Not with a plan. Just to move. To get out and stretch my legs and arms and maybe feel a little sun or breeze on my face. To be somewhere that didn't feel like it was waiting for me to figure something out.

I took the same route I always do, past the same places I've passed a hundred times without thinking much about them. The café was open as it usually is. I almost kept walking. But I didn't. I stepped inside instead. Ordered something small. Nothing I had to think about. Something familiar. They handed it to me with the same ease they always do, and I turned to leave before I noticed anything different.

"Wait—"

I paused.

They added a cup of coffee beside it. Set it down like it had always been part of the order. I started to say something, but they just smiled and waved it off before I could.

"On us today."

That was it. No explanation. No reason given.

Just... included.

I sat down because I had nowhere else to be. That was new. Usually I would have taken it to go. Kept moving. Folded it into the rest of the day without stopping long enough to notice it. But there was nothing waiting for me now. So I stayed.

The place felt different when I wasn't passing through it. Quieter. Not in sound, but in pace. People came and went. Conversations moved around me. Light shifted slowly across the table. And for the first time in a few days, I wasn't thinking about what had happened. Or what would come next. I was just there.

I sat there longer than I meant to. The cup had gone warm in my hands, but I didn't rush it. There wasn't anything waiting for me outside of that window. So I just sat and watched. At first, without really seeing.

Just movement. People coming and going, crossing paths without much thought. And then, slowly, it started to come into focus. A man held the door open longer than he needed to, his hand resting against it as someone hurried through with more in their arms than they could comfortably carry. Someone bent down near the trash can, picking up what had missed it without looking around to see if anyone had noticed.

A bus pulled up along the curb, and a woman stepped carefully down, one hand reaching for the rail, the other steadying herself. Someone behind her paused, not impatient, just waiting—giving her the space she needed to move at her own pace. A gust of wind caught the edge of someone's hat as they stepped off the sidewalk, lifting it just enough to carry it a few feet down the street. Another person reached out without thinking, catching it mid-step and handing it back before either of them had fully stopped moving.

Near the corner, someone handed a to-go box to a person sitting with all their belongings on the sidewalk, no words exchanged beyond a quiet thank you that didn't travel far.

None of it lasted more than a few seconds. None of it called attention to itself. And yet it kept happening. Small, steady moments. One after another. Not connected. But not separate either.

I hadn't been looking for any of it. If anything, I had been looking for the opposite. Something to confirm the way things had felt over the last few days. Something to match that narrowed view I had been carrying.

But it didn't.

The world outside that window didn't feel sharp or indifferent. It felt...human. Messy. Unplanned. Full of small adjustments made for one another without being asked.

I finished the last of the coffee and set the cup down gently, like it had been part of something more than just a stop in the day. When I stepped back outside, the air didn't feel different. But I did.

Not in a way that solved anything.

Just enough to notice more than I had before.

On the walk back, it stayed with me. Not as a single moment. But as a collection of them. Things I might have passed by any other day without seeing at all. A hand reaching out. A step slowed down. A space made where there hadn't been one before. Nothing that would have stood out on its own. But together, it shifted something.

It hadn't been that kindness wasn't there.

I just hadn't been looking for it.

I almost didn't stop. And if I hadn't, I might have carried that same narrow view a little longer. I might have missed the way the world was still moving around me in small, steady ways. Ways that didn't expect anything in return.

It didn't fix anything.

But it changed something.

And for that moment—

that was enough.

An Unplanned Journey

You hadn't planned to go into the forest.

You were walking to think, although thinking had felt increasingly like pacing lately—your phone warm in your hand, screen lighting up more often than you meant to look at it. Messages unanswered. Decisions deferred. The familiar pressure of needing to respond to something, someone, everything.

That's when the owl swooped low.

It moved silently, decisively, close enough that you startled—and before you could react, the phone was gone from your hand, lifted cleanly into the air.

"Hey—!"

The owl didn't slow. It didn't look back.

It vanished between the trees.

You stood there for a moment, heart racing, irritation flaring into disbelief. The urge to follow rose quickly, almost automatic. Then, without quite deciding to, you ran after it.

Beneath the trees, your breath slows before you notice why.

The forest does not announce itself. It simply closes around you.

Snow—or memory of it—falls away as you move deeper in. The light shifts, less demanding, more forgiving. You have the strange sense of being noticed, though nothing steps into your path.

High among the trunks, the stag stands motionless. Its breath rises in pale clouds. Nestled in the curve of its antlers, the owl watches—not urgently, but patiently. You understand, without knowing how, that it has already decided something about you—that you are ready to see, and that the forest has been waiting for this moment.

There is no urgency in this moment. You have the quiet sense that you are not late; you're right on time —that this threshold has been waiting for you.

You keep walking.

The path narrows, then loosens, then seems to stop insisting on being a path at all. You hesitate —uncertain, uncomfortable and not knowing which direction still counts as forward. For a moment, you consider turning back— you take a breath and let the feeling wash over you as though it is not apart of you and wait for it to fade away.

That is when the wolf appears.

He emerges from the mist at an easy pace, lantern swaying gently at his chest. The light is warm and steady, illuminating only what needs to be seen. He does not look back to check if you follow.

You do.

After a few steps, you notice something unexpected: you are no longer bracing for anything. It loosens, quietly, then slips away—as if the forest has asked you to stay awhile.

Time behaves differently deeper in the forest. The urgency that followed you in finds nothing to attach itself to. Moss thickens beneath your feet. The air smells damp and alive.

Something moves across the forest floor ahead of you—slow, deliberate.

A snail passes, carrying stone and moss upon its back. Worn arches are etched into its shell, softened by age, light seeping faintly from within. It does not hurry. It does not pause for you either.

The shell looks heavy, yet the snail does not strain. It carries only what belongs to it.

You slow without meaning to.

Somewhere behind you, the version of yourself everyone needs begins to loosen and fall away.

Near a pool of dark water, you stop.

A frog rests on a moss-covered stone. With each slow breath, a subtle pulse spreads outward into the water, into the ground, into you. Ripples form, steady and patient. Your breathing matches the rhythm before you think to change it.

You don't know how long you stand there. The rhythm you were keeping fades, replaced by something older... wiser...more ancient.

Further on, the forest opens into stillness.

The guardian is already there, shaped of bark and stone and leaf, seated as though the forest itself has chosen a place to rest. Moss covers him thickly. His presence asks nothing of you.

You sit.

At first, your thoughts keep moving. Then they begin to hush, and finally give way to quiet. You find yourself stopping, breathing, existing—without needing to justify it. When you stand again, the forest has not changed—your way of seeing it has.

At the edge of the trees, a raven perches on a fallen branch, feathers dark and matte. The raven watches the past, keeping it whole. Below, a hare stands in the dim light, a steady warmth glowing from within its small chest. The hare holds what remains—and what will continue—alive, present, waiting.

You realize that nothing needs to be undone for something new to begin. The past does not vanish, and the future does not arrive demanding proof. You are standing between them— unchanged in essence, yet no longer bound to move the way you once did.

Your phone lies at the base of the tree, dark and quiet. It rests in your hand, familiar—and yet less insistent than before. You don't turn it on. You slip it away, not as something lost and found, but as something that can wait.

Before leaving, you look once more at the forest—the stillness, the quiet continuity of it all. Snow begins to fall again at the edge of the trees, soft and unhurried. You step back toward the world beyond the forest, no longer carrying what was never yours to hold.

Behind you, the forest continues.

THE CAPTAIN'S CHOICE

The sea was calm when I understood we would not leave it as we were.

That is the lie of calm waters — they make you believe you have time. Time to mend a torn sail, time to argue, time to pray to whatever you once trusted. But the stillness that night had weight to it. The kind that settles only when the decision has already been made.

We had survived the storm, though the ship bore the truth of it. Timbers split where they should not have. A wound below the waterline that no hands could seal for long. The fog rolled in thick and close, pressing the world down to the length of our deck and no farther. No stars. No shore. Just us, and the quiet.

Ashbeard stood near the bow, still as if daring the sea to try him again. Old Rumjaw sat with his back against the mast, jaw clenched, counting breaths instead of rations. Silk Redmark worked a frayed line with careful fingers, precise even when there was no longer a point to precision. Edward the Seer had said nothing for hours, his eyes unfocused, as if he were already looking beyond the moment. And Vaelir — Vaelir listened. He always did. To the ship. To the water. To the spaces between what was said.

They waited for me.

A captain learns early that a crew can forgive many things — hunger, fear, even loss — but not hesitation. So when I spoke, I made sure my voice did not waver.

"There was a way," I told them. "A narrow one. The longboat could still be lowered. The wind, if it returned, might favor a few. Some of us could live."

For a long moment, no one spoke. Then Old Rumjaw cleared his throat. It was a small sound, but it carried.

"I always figured," he said slowly, eyes fixed on the dark water, "that one day I'd be fit for something on land."

Ashbeard let out a breath that might have been a laugh.

"And do what?" he asked quietly. "Stand still?"

Edward turned and faced us, as if waking from a thought he had been keeping to himself.

"I used to think I'd try my hand at farming," he said. Not hopeful. Just matter-of-fact.

Rumjaw glanced at him, this time with genuine curiosity.

"What would you grow?"

Edward considered this longer than he should have needed to.

"I never thought about it long enough," he said at last. "Didn't seem to matter."

Silk Redmark's hands paused on the line.

"That's how it always is," he said softly. "We picture the leaving. Never the staying."

The fog pressed closer. The ship creaked beneath us, familiar as breath.

"I was but a boy at my mother's knee," I said then, surprising even myself, "the first time I saw a sea captain. I knew then it was the only thing I'd ever be."

Vaelir's whisper moved through the fog, steady and sure.

"Some lives are only given one act."

No one answered that. They didn't need to. Rumjaw nodded once, slow and settled, as if something long unspoken had finally found its place. And in that silence, I understood — We had only said aloud what we already knew. If we lived, we would not become different men. We would find another ship, another crew, another reason to keep doing the "leaving". The sea would take its due later, as it always does. Survival would only delay the ending, not change it.

I felt the choice settle fully into my bones then. Survival that asks you to pretend you are someone else is not survival at all. It is merely a performance.

So I told them the rest. I told them how I would not command a future that required abandoning even one soul who had trusted me with their life. That if the sea meant to claim us, it would take us together — not in panic, not in pieces, but as we had lived: bound by oath and choice.

Ashbeard laughed, low and fierce, as if I had spoken something obvious at last. Old Rumjaw spat over the side and nodded once. Silk tied off his line and stood, ready. Edward met my eyes, and in his gaze I saw no fear — only recognition. Vaelir's whisper reached me last, carried on the damp air.

"I thought so", he said. Or perhaps he did not say it aloud at all.

We did not pray. We did not fight the sea. We simply remained. The water rose without anger. Cold, yes — but not cruel. The ship groaned as if relieved of a long burden, settling deeper, deeper still. I remember thinking, with a strange clarity, that this was how it must feel to finally set something heavy down.

There was no darkness. When the deck slipped beneath the surface, we did not sink as men do. The sea took the weight from us, not the will. Breath became unnecessary. Pain loosened its grip. And though the world changed, we did not disappear. We stayed. We became something between — not living, not lost. Bound to the water, but no longer claimed by it. We do not yet know why we remain. Only that we were not meant to scatter, or to fade, or to be done. The sea has always revealed its truths in time. And when ours is shown, we will see it through, as we always have — together, and without turning away.

For now, we sail the quiet waters.

We keep watch.

We endure.

And that, for the moment, is enough.

THE LONG WHILE

Some relationships don't arrive with beginnings so much as they simply exist, already shaped by proximity and time. They take form slowly, without ceremony, until one day you realize they have been part of your life for years, woven into the ordinary pattern of days without ever asking to be named.

This was one of those relationships. Two houses set within sight of one another, close enough to share weather and seasons, far enough apart that neither required much of the other. A fence ran between the properties, more suggestion than boundary, its boards weathered by years of wind and quiet neglect.

The board had slipped again sometime over the winter. It wasn't dramatic—just enough to catch the eye when spring came and the light changed. It would have been easy to leave it as it was. No one would have noticed. No one would have expected anything different.

Still, one morning, the board was lifted back into place. The work took only a few minutes. A nail pulled straight. A hammer set down. Nothing was said, because there was no one there to say it to.

Later that day, the neighbor stood on their side of the fence for a long moment. Their gaze lingered on the repaired board, then moved away again. They did not cross the distance between the houses. They did not call out. Life continued, as it always had.

It wasn't the last time something small presented itself.

One summer afternoon, the mailbox lay tipped into the grass, its post loosened and the earth around it disturbed. It was easy enough to guess what had happened—nothing intentional, just the careless momentum of someone passing through. By evening, it stood straight again, the dirt packed firm around its base, the hinge checked and set right.

The next morning, the flag was raised.

After that, the years settled into one another. The houses remained. The fence held. There were winters that came hard and summers that lingered longer than expected. The relationship did not deepen, but it did not disappear either. It simply continued, shaped by the same quiet distance it had always known. When small moments arose—nothing urgent, nothing dramatic—the choice returned. Sometimes it was honored. Sometimes it was weighed first, then honored anyway. Not because it changed anything between them, but because it preserved something within.

The winter that followed was a heavy one. Snow came early and stayed late, pressing the landscape flat and quiet. After one storm in particular, the road disappeared entirely, and the driveways had to be reclaimed by hand. The neighbor's drive was long. Clearing all of it would have taken the better part of the morning. Instead, a narrow path appeared—just wide enough for a car to pass, just enough to make leaving possible if leaving was needed. The rest remained untouched, smooth and white, as though nothing had disturbed it at all.

By the time the neighbor came out, the shovel was already put away. There was no wave. No call across the snow. Only the sound of boots on packed ground and the quiet continuation of the day.

Time altered things in small, unavoidable ways. Strength waned. Mornings took longer. What once cost only a few minutes began to require thought. The choices did not disappear, but they asked more clearly to be considered.

By then, the kindness had found its shape. It did not announce itself, and it did not reach beyond what could be sustained. When a bag split at the edge of the drive one autumn afternoon, the help offered was brief and practical—hands gathering what had spilled, weight lifted only once, then set down again.

The neighbor nodded. The moment passed.

In the later years, there was less to notice. Fewer small repairs. Fewer moments that asked for decision. The fence held. The mailbox stayed upright. Winters still came, but they were met differently now, with shorter paths and longer rests.

The neighbor moved more slowly. Some days, they did not come outside at all. When they did, it was briefly—standing on the porch, leaning more heavily than they once had, as though measuring whether the effort of stepping down was worth the cost. Sometimes it was. Often, it wasn't.

That summer, the grass nearest the road was cut back once, just enough to keep it from spilling into the drive. No more than that. The rest was left as it was, uneven and growing wild. The next time the neighbor stood on the porch, their gaze rested on the cleared strip for a moment before turning away.

After that, there were fewer moments still. The porch stayed empty even on mild days. The yard went untended entirely. Mail collected longer in the box before being taken in, then not at all. The absence settled in, not sudden enough to alarm, but steady enough to be felt. Eventually, there was no one left to notice. The house stood quiet through a full turn of seasons, unchanged from the road except for the stillness that entered it and stayed.

It was a relative who came eventually, someone distant enough to move through the house with efficiency rather than familiarity. The work took a day, maybe two. Doors were opened. Drawers emptied. Things were sorted into what could be kept and what could not.

The box appeared near the end. It was medium in size, neatly closed, set apart from the rest. A name was written on the lid in careful, deliberate handwriting. The relative hesitated when they brought it over, holding it out with both hands.

"You're Andrew, right?" they asked quietly.

He nodded.

"We found this in a drawer at my uncle's house," they said. "It had your name on it."

Nothing more was added. There didn't seem to be anything else that needed saying. The relative gave a small, polite smile, then turned back toward the quiet house.

Andrew carried the box inside and set it on the table by the window. Afternoon light gathered there, soft and familiar, settling into the grain of the wood.

He waited longer than he meant to before opening it. The house moved around him—coffee cooling, a door closing somewhere down the hall, the ordinary sounds of a life still in motion.

Inside were several watercolor paintings on paper, stacked carefully, their corners softened and edges worn thin with handling. Thin sheets had been placed between them once, though time had made those nearly translucent.

The first showed the fence, decades earlier, its boards newly set straight, light falling across it in uneven bands. Another captured the mailbox standing upright against a wide summer sky, grass pressed down at its base. There was the narrow path through snow, pale and deliberate, cutting cleanly through the white.

Beneath them was one larger sheet. It showed a yard in late afternoon—it was Andrew's yard. Children ran through a sprinkler, their movement blurred into color and light. A shaggy dog streaked past them, all legs and joy. The moment was unposed, ordinary, and unmistakably his.

Andrew recognized the day not by its date, but by the feeling of it—the kind of happiness that doesn't announce itself, the kind you only realize later mattered.

At the bottom of the box was a single folded note. The paper was softened by time, the handwriting careful and slightly uneven.

Thank you for being kind.

I saw more than I knew how to say.

It was good to live beside you.

Andrew closed the box and sat down. Outside, the light shifted—just slightly—and he understood something he had never needed to know before. He had spent years noticing what the neighbor required, responding in the only ways he could. Only now did he realize that he, too, had been seen—held in another's attention, observed with care, known in a language different from his own